*Dedicated to the memory of
LCpl. Christopher B. Cosgrove III
and all the selfless Americans
who have given their lives to protect
our Freedom over the years.*

PROLOGUE

This is not good, thought Christopher as he looked around him. Smoke lingered in the air from the mortars and gunfire aimed at the landing fleet. Suddenly, the cold water of the English Channel drenched him and the other men in their landing craft when a German shell exploded next to them as they headed for Omaha Beach, Normandy, France. It was June 6, 1944.

The screaming noise of incoming shells sounded like a train soaring overhead. The "ack-ack-ack" of the machine guns strategically placed on the bluff above the beach was deafening. The putrid smell of burning oil and the constant sound of ammunition exploding clearly indicated that the Omaha Beach landing was a disaster—and Christopher's group was due to land there in minutes. Just then, the landing craft next to theirs disintegrated when it was hit with a German mortar, killing everyone onboard.

Christopher looked over at Kevin and Brian, his fellow "Fighting Hawks." Trying to hide the fear etched on their faces, they glanced around to see if everyone else was as scared as they were. They had aged ten years in just the past few minutes. Christopher wondered if he would ever see them again.

Wags, Will, and Jack had parachuted into Normandy earlier this morning. Had they survived the death-defying jump? He had been down this path before, and the only outcome that was certain was that people died: good, decent people. Christopher's last thoughts before the landing-craft ramp dropped were of his family back home in New Jersey, sleeping peacefully in their warm beds. *Whatever happens, it's worth it,* he thought.

Suddenly, the boatswain driving the landing craft screamed over the noise of the guns and explosions. "We're going in! Get ready!" The ship surged toward the beach.

In an instant, the heavy metal ramp at the front of the craft dropped quickly, exposing all the men to incoming German machine-gun fire. The men at the front of the craft started dropping immediately, killed instantly by incoming bullets.

"Get over the side *now!*" screamed Christopher as he launched himself into the water. Kevin and Brian quickly followed him overboard.

Grabbing Brian from under the water, Christopher scrambled to dodge bullets and get behind a nearby German obstacle strategically placed to block the Allied invasion. As he surveyed the bloody scene in front of him, he thought, *Oh my God, we've landed in hell! How did I get here?*

CHAPTER ONE

Military History Class

It was a damp, overcast day at Parris Island, South Carolina—the kind of day United States Marine recruits hated. Marine Recruit Christopher Cosgrove had already been up since 4:00 a.m., hiking fifteen miles while carrying an eighty-pound backpack. He was twenty years old, spending the summer between his junior and senior year at Monmouth University at Marine boot camp. Christopher was a scrappy guy, standing five-feet-eleven-inches tall, 170 pounds, with dark-brown hair before the marines had shaved it off on his arrival at Parris Island four days earlier.

Today was the first day of his military history class.

"Hey Coz, wait up!" BJ said, racing to catch up to him.

Christopher turned to see B. J. Gianni, all six feet of him, running toward him with his notebook in hand.

"You ready for our first class?" BJ said excitedly. "I was never very good at history, but I think I'll enjoy learning about the battles that kept us free!"

"BJ, I've been studying military history for as long as I can remember," Christopher said. "I'm more afraid I'm going to fall asleep during class. *That* would not be good!"

"Really?" BJ said, surprised at his response. "How'd you get into military history?"

"My grandfather was a POW during World War II. Plus, when I was young, I used to go all over to see historic landmarks and battlefields. It was pretty interesting, especially when they did the reenactments. After that, I started reading about them," Christopher said.

"This class should be a piece of cake for you! Just sit back and relax while the rest of us struggle through it!" replied BJ.

"Maybe, but the last thing I need is to listen to Sergeant Carney lecture me for two hours on military history," said Christopher.

"Well, at least the building won't be so hot today," BJ said encouragingly.

As Christopher and BJ took their seats in the classroom, Sgt. Carney began to speak. His voice was soft and soothing, unlike the drill sergeant and other marines he had dealt with over the past few days.

While BJ furiously scribbled notes, Christopher tried to focus. Prone to distraction, he found the soothing voice did not help. Still, Christopher tried to concentrate as Sgt. Carney explained how the war began.

"The world was at war. It started brewing slowly. Japan began the war by invading China to its west, in July 1937. In March 1938, Nazi Germany, led by Adolf Hitler, invaded eastern Europe, starting with Austria. By September 1938, the Sudetenland of Czechoslovakia was ceded to Germany without objection from either Britain or France. In March 1939, Hitler took over the rest of Czechoslovakia. All these countries were taken over without a shot fired or the loss of a single German life. As a result, Germany gained not only strategic territory—granting Hitler the ability to dominate southern Europe—but, also, put ten million people under the control of Nazi Germany. These countries had tremendous resources Germany could use in their crusade to conquer Europe. Britain and France realized their mistake and declared war on Germany in September 1939," Sgt. Carney said.

As Sgt. Carney droned on about D-Day, Christopher gazed out the window. Suddenly, a fierce wind blew the fluttering American flag. As Christopher watched the blowing flag, a portal opened and the battle took shape right before his eyes…

CHAPTER TWO

Meeting Old Friends

It was May 29, 1944. The military leaders of the Allied Forces (American and British) and their troops had been planning and training for this invasion for more than a year. There was no doubt that the D-Day invasion at Normandy would determine the future of the world. Hitler had to be defeated.

Christopher, as a member of the 116th Infantry Division, was designated to land on Omaha Beach at Normandy. Christopher and his buddies Kevin White and Brian Donnelly could not wait to go. They were tired of training for the invasion—they were ready and wanted to fight. They understood the importance of defeating Germany and restoring freedom in Europe.

Christopher had enlisted while attending Monmouth University in New Jersey. He was five-foot-eleven-inches tall, 170 pounds, had dark brown hair, and he had the longest eyelashes anyone had ever seen. Girls loved them. Having already fought in several battles in North Africa, he knew this invasion was going to be difficult because of the landing site's geography. The Germans had a distinct advantage over the Allied Forces. However, he prided himself on his ability to remain calm in the face of danger, often using humor to cut the tension of his fellow soldiers.

Kevin White, just nineteen years old, had enlisted right after he graduated from St. Peter's Preparatory School in Jersey City, New Jersey. His Jesuit education had instilled in him the importance of being a "Man for Others." He felt compelled to serve others and make the world a better place. Three inches taller and only ten pounds heavier than Christopher, Kevin viewed himself as a "lean, mean fighting machine." Kevin's physical prowess was matched by his brains.

Brian Donnelly was only seventeen years old. Despite being the smallest of the three at five-foot-ten-inches tall and just 145 pounds, Brian was incredibly strong and fast.

He was also the most analytical. He and Kevin met at the enlistment office. Motivated by Brian's unending energy and determination, and impressed by his dedication to the service, Kevin became like a big brother to Brian when they went off to boot camp. He liked the way Kevin looked after him.

They arrived in England in March 1944 and were assigned to the same unit as Christopher. Kevin and Christopher hit it off right away. They had the same wacky sense of humor as well as respect for country. They came from similar backgrounds and felt as if they had known each other forever. Brian was the quiet one, pensive and obsessed with detail. He needed a plan. If he didn't have a plan, he could come up with one quickly and was very good at improvising. This trait would prove to be both annoying and invaluable when they landed on Omaha Beach. Christopher knew that and respected him as a soldier. Christopher saw a lot of himself in Brian.

Christopher, Kevin, and Brian went out to dinner at a local pub in England a few weeks before they boarded the ship for the Normandy invasion. The dimly lit pub was filled with soldiers preparing to deploy. Smoke filled the air as music played softly in the background. Some of the soldiers were on dates with local girls, while others were sitting at the bar trying to meet women.

Christopher, Kevin, and Brian found a table in the corner of the room. As they sat there, someone smacked Kevin in the back of the head.

Kevin jumped up yelling, "What the…!"

As he turned around, he saw C. J. Wagsley. He was Kevin's best friend from elementary school. They had been friends since third grade but had lost touch.

"Hey, Kev! Fancy meeting you here!" exclaimed Wags, happy to see his old friend.

Kevin grabbed him in a bear hug. "What a great surprise! What are you doing here?" Kevin asked.

"I'm a member of the Screaming Eagles, the 101st Airborne," Wags said proudly.

Kevin introduced Wags to Christopher and Brian, and invited him to join them for dinner. Wags agreed but told Kevin he was also with friends and wanted them to join him.

"Will, come over here!" Wags yelled, waving over one of his friends.

As Will walked through the crowd, Kevin couldn't believe his eyes.

"Oh my God! How do you guys know each other?" Kevin asked as he gave Will a firm handshake.

"We're in the same stick in the 101st," Wags said. "How do you know Will?"

"Kev and I went to St. Peter's Prep together," Will said.

Kevin then introduced Will to Christopher and Brian, explaining that he had met Brian at the enlistment office and Christopher when he got to England.

"Nice to meet you," Christopher and Brian said, almost in unison, as they stood to shake Will's hand.

"Same here," Will said politely, extending his hand to Christopher and Brian. "Any friend of Kevin's is a friend of mine."

Will turned to Wags and asked, "Where's Jack?"

"Over there, flirting with the pretty waitress again," Wags said.

"Jack, get over here," Will said, waving him over. "Meet our friends!"

As Jack walked over, Brian was dumbfounded. He hadn't seen his friend Jack since they graduated a year earlier.

"Jack! What are you doing here?" Brian said, jumping up to shake his hand.

"The 101st Airborne, with Wags and Will," Jack answered. "What about you?"

"We're with the 116th Infantry," introducing Kevin and Christopher.

"Glad to meet you," Jack said as they sat down.

Jack waved the tall brunette waitress over to get their dinner order. Wags, Will, and Jack sat down at the round wooden table and shared stories about their antics with Kevin and Brian when they were young.

"I'm starting to feel left out," Christopher said, laughing.

"Don't," said Wags, "it sounds a lot better now than it did at the time. We're lucky we're still here."

As they waited for their dinner, Christopher and Wags talked about the history of the war so far. Being the youngest of the group, Brian and Jack were intrigued because they had not paid much attention to world events while in high school. They had been more interested in getting their homework and chores done and going to the movies with some of the girls they knew.

"So let me get this straight," stated Brian, "Germany invaded Poland on September 1, 1939, even after they agreed with Britain and France that they would leave Poland alone?"

"Exactly," Christopher replied. "They engaged in a method of warfare they call 'blitzkrieg,' or 'lightening war.'"

"What's that?" Jack asked curiously.

"German air attacks destroy the invaded country's air force before it can get airborne, as well as their railroads, roads, and ammunition dumps. Then, they shoot the soldiers and fleeing civilians as they try to escape," declared Christopher.

"That's brilliant! Evil—but brilliant!" exclaimed Brian, listening intently.

"It's a very effective method of warfare. Tanks and light armored vehicles then rapidly invade on the ground, capturing a lot of territory, with the infantry following behind. There isn't much the target country can do to stop them," Christopher said.

"I bet the British and French leaders felt like idiots," Jack said in disbelief. "How could they have trusted Hitler?"

"After the death and destruction in World War I, no one wanted to get into another global war, so they tried to appease him, hoping he would stop. By September 3, 1939, France and Britain realized they had made a terrible mistake, and they declared war on Germany. Unfortunately, it was too late," Christopher said, shaking his head.

"Why?" Brian asked.

Will jumped into the conversation: "Because Hitler was bound and determined to destroy the Polish and Jewish races, as well as the sick and disabled. In fact, he wanted to destroy every race except the Aryan race, which he deemed to be the perfect race. He viewed the Aryan race as a people with a combination of Nordic features, pure German ancestry, strength, and courage."

"Once Hitler took over Poland, he ordered the German army to begin mass killings of the Polish and Jewish people, along with the infirm and disabled. Thousands of innocent people were killed each day. Ironically, the Japanese were doing the same thing on the other side of the world," declared Christopher.

"Oh my God!" Jack said, clearly disgusted.

"Anyway," Christopher continued, "Hitler continued his march across Europe. Between April and June 1940, Germany invaded and captured Belgium, Holland, France, and Luxembourg using his blitzkrieg tactics."

Joining the conversation, Kevin continued the history lesson. "Italian dictator Benito Mussolini decided to join Hitler's war effort and declared war on Britain and France. When he did this, he extended the war into the British and French territories in North Africa."

"So now, most of Europe, including France, is under Hitler's control, and the British and French need to protect their territories in North Africa too?" Brian asked in disbelief.

"Yup. And it gets worse," Christopher said. "In August 1940, Hitler began bombing Great Britain on a daily basis, trying to force them to surrender. Luckily, the British refused to give up. In fact, within a short period of time, the Germans had lost half their air force because the British planes were better than the German planes. Also, the British had set up a very effective radar and air defense system that gave them advance warning. Radar enabled the British pilots to ambush the German planes and pilots on the bombing raids."

"So that's why there are a lot of bombed-out buildings in England," Jack stated. "I was wondering about that."

"When you hear the Brits talk about the 'Battle of Britain,' that's what they're referring to," Will said, surprised at how little Brian and Jack knew about why they were there.

"It is fortunate for the British that Hitler decided to suspend his campaign against Great Britain when he did. He was very close to succeeding when he shifted gears and decided to overtake the Soviet Union to his east," continued Christopher.

"I don't understand why it took so long for the United States to get involved?" Brian said.

"We didn't want to get involved for the same reason France and Britain appeased Hitler. We lost a lot of men in World War I, and we did not want to get involved in another war. Slowly, as the situation worsened, we began sending weapons and supplies to Britain to aid their war effort. Still, the American people believed we didn't have to send men because we were protected by the Atlantic Ocean to the east and the Pacific Ocean to the west," replied Christopher. "But all that changed on December 7, 1941…"

"When the Japanese bombed Pearl Harbor," Jack said, finishing Christopher's thought for him.

"That's right," said Christopher. "We lost over two thousand men in that sneak attack, and they destroyed or disabled most of our naval fleet in the Pacific. Anyway, we declared war on Japan on December 8, 1941, and Germany declared war on us on December 13. Suddenly, we were at war on two fronts."

"Japan in the Pacific, and Germany and Italy in the Atlantic," Brian said proudly.

"After the attack on Pearl Harbor, the Japanese began to take over British and American territories in the Pacific in countless bloody battles. We've been fighting alongside the British in Africa and Italy, but in order to defeat Hitler and win this war, we've got to invade Europe. That's why we're all here," said Christopher matter-of-factly.

Just then, the waitress arrived with their dinner. The conversation turned to talk about the mission and their responsibilities.

"What's a 'stick'?" asked Brian inquisitively, referring to how Wags, Will and Jack met.

"It's a group of 18 men who jump and train together," said Will.

"So, what kind of training have you guys been doing?" Christopher asked.

"A lot of jumps, running with equipment, target practice, and a couple of training exercises that lasted a few days each. They just decided to give us leg bags last week. They should come in handy," replied Wags.

"What are 'leg bags'?" asked Kevin.

"They're bags that attach to our leg. The Brits have been using them for a while. They can hold extra equipment, ammo, radios and stuff. They're attached to our legs by twenty foot cords, so once our chutes deploy, we can release the bag, and it'll drop down but stay attached to us. It will hit the ground first so we can roll properly when we land. It's really just extra storage space for our gear," Will said.

"How about you guys?" asked Jack.

"We've done some practice landing exercises on the English beaches, but I'm ready for the real thing!" Brian said.

"Me too!" said Kevin excitedly.

Christopher shook his head and leaned over to Wags. "They have no idea what they're in for."

"None of us do—except you," said Wags. "You've suddenly gone quiet. Is that why?"

"No. I'm just taking it all in," Christopher replied. "It'll be a long time before we get to do this again...if ever."

"I know," said Wags pensively. "How bad is it?"

"You will see and do things you never wanted to," answered Christopher, "but in the end, you need to remember, our mission is just. That will make it easier to understand."

"I'm not sure I can shoot someone," said Wags reluctantly.

"When the time comes, where it's you, one of your buddies, or them, you'll be able to," Christopher said. "Trust me."

"I hope you're right," replied Wags.

They turned back to the lively conversation at the table.

After dinner, Wags looked at his watch and finished his drink. "Time to go Screaming Eagles," said Wags.

Will and Jack finished their drinks and stood up to go. Christopher and Kevin started to get ready to leave as well. Brian, however, was curious about the nickname "Screaming Eagles."

"Hey Wags, how'd the 101st Airborne get such a great nickname?" asked Brian as he stood to say good-bye.

"The nickname comes from our division's insignia, which has a bald eagle on a black shield," stated Wags. "It's actually pretty famous."

"Good luck Wags," said Brian as he shook his hand. "See you in Paris."

"You too, Brian," said Wags. "I'm looking forward to it."

Wags, Will, and Kevin wished each other well and said their good-byes.

"Stay safe, Wags, Will," said Kevin.

"You, too, man. We'll meet up in France," laughed Wags.

"Can't wait!" said Kevin.

In the meantime, Jack and Brian reminisced about their days as "Hawks" football players. "I can't believe it's been so long since we've seen each other—and we meet here," said Brian.

"We had a lot of fun times," laughed Jack. "I'll see you soon."

"Sounds good!" replied Brian as he shook Jack's hand.

After Wags, Will, and Jack left the pub, Brian sat back down and looked at Christopher and Kevin.

"I want a nickname too," Brian said.

"You've got to be kidding me," said Kevin. "We're about to launch the biggest invasion in the history of the world, and you're worried about a nickname?"

"No, really, I'm serious," Brian said with a determined look on his face. Kevin knew when Brian gave him that look there was no point in arguing with him.

"Actually, I like the idea, too. It makes us a team," stated Christopher. Brian was definitely growing on him. "What should we call ourselves?"

Kevin sighed, "Well, I was a 'Marauder' in high school."

Brian looked at Kevin. "I don't really think we want to be known as pirates when we invade France," said Brian, rolling his eyes.

"Good point," said Christopher. "For what it's worth, I was a 'Hawk' in college."

"Really?" asked Brian. "I was a 'Hawk' in elementary school."

Kevin sat there looking at Christopher and Brian, shaking his head.

"All right. Hawks are strong and free. They have great eyesight and swoop down on their prey, just like we're going to do to the Germans. We're 'Hawks'!" declared Kevin, thinking he pacified Brian.

Christopher and Brian thought about it for a while. Finally, Brian said, "No, that's not good enough."

Christopher watched Brian as he stuck his tongue out of the side of his mouth while he was thinking.

Come to think of it, he does it when he's fighting too, thought Christopher.

"I've got it. We're the '*Fighting* Hawks'!" declared Christopher triumphantly.

Brian and Kevin smiled. "That's it! From here on out, we're the 'Fighting Hawks.' Now, let's get out of here. We've got a long few weeks ahead of us," said Kevin.

They paid the bill and left, leaving a large tip for the pretty waitress.

CHAPTER THREE

On Our Way, the Invasion Begins

On May 31, 1944, the troops began boarding the ships that would take them to the area of Normandy Beach. Christopher, Kevin, and Brian—the "Fighting Hawks"—boarded their transport ship on the afternoon of June 1, 1944. Their ship was one of more than five thousand that carried the 156,000 troops, tanks, supplies, and equipment to support the invasion. On those transport ships were more than twenty-seven hundred smaller boats, known as Higgins boats, which would bring the men and equipment from the larger transport ships to shore on the day of the invasion. Seventy-five convoys traveled from southern England to Normandy Beach on the French coast for the invasion.[i]

"I don't get it," said Brian. "What sense does it make for us to land in Normandy, especially Omaha Beach? We have to cross heavily fortified beaches and scale steep slopes while being shot at by Germans. There's got to be a better way!" he exclaimed.

Kevin, clearly frustrated, looked at Christopher. "Can you please explain it to him? He doesn't understand the plan when I explain it."

"Look, Bri, it's really not that complicated," said Christopher, pulling out his map. "Since the German army controls the Atlantic wall—meaning the entire coastline from Norway to Denmark, the Netherlands, Belgium, France, and the Bay of Biscay—General Eisenhower had to figure out the best way to invade Europe."

"But why Normandy?" asked Brian.

"I'm not sure," said Christopher, "but I expect he wants to use the element of surprise. Also, Omaha Beach is very wide at low tide. It will give us a lot of room to unload our troops and supplies. I doubt there will be much resistance by the time we get there."

Kevin jumped in. "You see, Brian, if we invade France directly across the English Channel at Pas de Calais, it would be a massacre. The Germans are highly fortified in that area because that's where they expect us to attack."

Kevin continued, "Have you noticed all of the bombing raids our pilots have been conducting lately? They're trying to take out the bridges, railroads and roads inland, as well as their oil refineries, so the Germans can't get to the beaches."

"Maybe, but I'm still not crazy about this plan," said Brian.

Christopher looked at Brian and smiled. "None of us are," he said, "but General Eisenhower is nobody's fool. You'll see when we get out there that he has everything covered."

Brian shook his head reluctantly as they set sail for Normandy. The invasion was scheduled for June 5, 1944.

At 4:00 a.m. on June 4, Gen. Eisenhower was at Southwick House, the Allied Forces headquarters in Portsmouth, England. He was advised that there would be hurricane-force winds, rain, low clouds, and four-foot surf along the French coast on June 5. Gen. Eisenhower decided to delay the invasion for one day. The ships stopped their advance toward the Normandy Beaches, and, instead, held off for another day. Many of the men became seasick as the ships rolled violently on the high waves. Luckily for the Allied Forces, the German air force was also grounded because of the bad weather, so they did not see the impending invasion force.

Christopher, Kevin, and Brian spent June 5 cleaning and re-cleaning their rifles and playing cards. Eating was out of the question—the ship was being tossed around in the English Channel like a toy boat in a bathtub.

Later that evening, they received their final briefing from their commander. Pulling out the aerial photos of Omaha Beach, Major Martin explained the terrain to the men.

"When you land, you'll need to get across roughly three hundred yards of open yellow sand. Next, you'll get to the shingle, which is an area of very slippery rock. Once you get over the shingle, you'll encounter the three-foot seawall. Next, get to the exits off the beach—the tanks will have cleared the way by the time you get there. Follow the men ahead of you up the draw (path) to the bluff on top of the beach. Remember, there will be German obstacles all over the beach and minefields around the draws. If you get into trouble, use these obstacles for cover."

Afterward, Christopher gathered Kevin and Brian. "Listen guys, no matter what happens tomorrow, we have to get over the shingle, find the draw and get up the bluff," said Christopher. "If we get pinned down by German machine gun fire, we're dead meat, and I, for one, intend to get home to my family."

Brian looked at Christopher skeptically. "I thought you said General Eisenhower had all angles covered?"

"This is the military," replied Kevin. "Nothing ever goes exactly as planned. Our superiors do their best, but we need to be able to improvise. Our lives may depend on it."

Christopher pulled out his map to go over it one more time with Kevin and Brian.

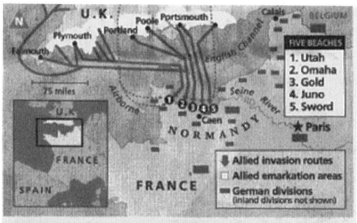

D-Day
June 6, 1944

■ Term signifying a military operation start date, now identified with the invasion of Europe by U.S. Allied forces on June 6, 1944

■ Actual name of invasion was Operation Overlord

■ The Nazis believed the invasion would occur at the narrowest spot on the English Channel

■ The invasion actually focused on five beaches on the coast of Normandy, France.

■ The five beaches were code-named Utah, Omaha, Gold, Juno and Sword

■ 176,000 Allied soldiers stormed the beaches, the largest sea-borne invasion in history

■ Allied casualties totaled 11,000 (including 2,500 dead)

■ Considered the turning point of the War in Europe

"Remember, there will be more than one hundred fifty thousand men landing on the Normandy beaches which cover a distance of fifty miles. They are divided into five sectors, west to east: Utah, Omaha, Gold, Juno, and Sword. The British will land on Sword and Gold. The Canadians and some Brits at Juno. The Americans at Omaha and Utah," said Christopher.

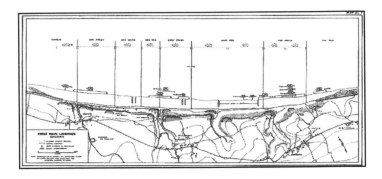

Kevin pulled the map between him and Brian. "Brian, we're landing here," pointing to Omaha Beach. "We are not in the first three waves to hit the beach so, if all goes well, we'll just follow the infantry ahead of us."

"What do you mean *if* all goes well?" asked Brian.

"Okay, Brian, one more time," said Christopher. "The Allied Air Forces have been continuously bombing inland roads, bridges, and railroads to prevent the Germans from reinforcing the beaches to stop us. Plus, when this invasion officially begins, twenty-four thousand Allied troops will be landing in France behind enemy lines by way of gliders and paratroopers. Sixteen thousand of them will be from the 101st and the 82nd Airborne Divisions, including Wags, Will, and Jack."

Kevin jumped in. "They are going to secure very important roads and bridges over the Douve and Orne rivers; and towns such as Pouppeville, Saint Martin, and Saint-Germain to prevent a German counterattack against the landing Allied Forces. As we launch the sea invasion on the beaches at Normandy, more than ten thousand Allied bombers[ii] and fighter planes will be dropping thousands of bombs on the coastline to take out whatever obstacles, mines, pillboxes, and soldiers are waiting for us on the beaches. Plus, amphibious divisions will land before any of our troops to take out any remaining German soldiers."

Brian studied the map carefully and looked at Christopher and Kevin. "Do you have a plan to get to the draw and up the bluff if things don't go as planned?" he asked.

Christopher and Kevin looked at Brian, shrugged their shoulders and said simultaneously, "We'll improvise."

"Wrong," exclaimed Brian. "Let's at least try to come up with a plan, just in case."

Kevin and Christopher looked at Brian. "We're listening," Christopher stated intensely.

"All right," said Brian. "You said there are obstacles on the beach, right?"

Christopher and Kevin nodded affirmatively.

"Well, in the worst case scenario, we'll need to use those obstacles for cover. They're about five to six feet tall and made of steel beams. That means they will deflect bullets. By the time we get onto the beach, there will probably be some vehicles stuck on the beach, too, right?"

Again, Christopher and Kevin nodded affirmatively.

"If we're taking fire, find cover behind whatever you can. And whatever happens, we need to stay together. Once we've found cover, we can come up with a plan from there. After all, we're the Fighting Hawks, right?" asked Brian. "Agreed?"

"Agreed!" said Christopher and Kevin.

CHAPTER FOUR

Launching the Air Invasion

As Christopher and Kevin explained the invasion to Brian, the British and American paratroopers prepared for takeoff to start the air invasion. C. J. "Wags" Wagsley, Will Browning, and Jack Hart were members of the elite 101st Airborne Division—also known as the "Screaming Eagles". They were part of the 506th Parachute Infantry Regiment.

Wags, standing six-feet-four-inches tall and weighing 220 pounds, was nineteen years old. Quiet and smart, Wags generally kept to himself until he got to know a person. Wags had enlisted right after high school. Jack, on the other hand, was six inches shorter and sixty pounds lighter than Wags. Having grown up on a farm in New Jersey, Jack was extremely fit and strong, as well as quite personable. Will, a college boy, was six-feet-two-inches tall and weighed 165 pounds. Will was a two-sport athlete at Stanford University in California, playing quarterback on the football team and swimming, before he'd enlisted.

Preparing for the invasion, Wags, Jack, and Will smeared charcoal on their faces and hands to camouflage themselves. Because they would be landing behind enemy lines, their ability to remain undetected was imperative to the mission. All of the paratroopers were busy doing the same thing. Once they were done with the charcoal, they checked each other's equipment to make sure it was secure.

"Let's do an equipment check," said Jack. "Do you guys have the fifty pounds of two-and-a-half pound explosives, the fuses, primer cord, blasting caps, and the detonator for the three ten-pound antitank mines?" asked Jack.

Both Wags and Will yelled, "Yes!"

"Wags, do you have the flamethrower and fuel?" Jack asked.

"Unfortunately! You guys are lucky you don't have to carry this extra weight." replied Wags.

"What about your gun and extra ammo?" asked Jack.

"Got it," they both replied.

"How many grenades do you each have?" questioned Jack.

"I've got six hand grenades, plus I've got my forty-five-caliber pistol and fifty rounds of ammunition," said Will. "What about you, Wags?"

"Same," declared Wags.

"Where are your knives?" asked Will.

I've got three knives: one on my leg, one on my ankle, and one in my collar area," indicated Jack. "Wags?"

"Me too," said Wags. "Not that I can get to them with all this stuff on."

"Everybody got their 'cricket clicker'?" asked Jack, playing with the metal child's toy that made cricket-like clicking noises. "It may keep us from getting killed by friendly fire."

"Got it," they both declared.

"Alright, we all have our parachutes and reserve chutes, right?" asked Wags.

"Obviously," indicated Jack.

"K rations, rope, flashlight, shovel, field glasses, water, life preserver, French francs, first-aid kits with morphine, and condoms in your leg bags?" asked Will.

"And the condoms are for what again?" questioned Jack.

"They're good for keeping our weapons clean. Put it over the top of the gun barrel to keep mud and sand out. Plus, if you need to fire your gun, the bullet will go right through it," answered Wags. "Remember?"

As they walked toward their plane, Will turned to Wags and Jack and yelled over the roar of the plane engines, "Can you believe how many planes there are?"

Wags laughed, "I wouldn't want to be the Germans watching these planes come in."

Jack looked at them both and said, "Hey guys, don't get too cocky. They're going to be shooting at us on the way down. We'll be sitting ducks until we hit the ground."

"Maybe," said Will, "but there are more than eight hundred twenty C-47 planes and twenty-four thousand men here. They can't get all of us!"

"Did you hear them say in our briefing that the planes will be flying in a nine-wide formation, and that the line of planes will be three hundred miles long before we're all dropped? That's going to be an intimidating sight!" said Wags confidently.

The planes were loaded with equipment bundles underneath and in the doorway of the plane. These bundles contained extra supplies such as ammunition, bazookas, military radios, cigarettes, and food.

A few hours earlier, a small number of pathfinder troops had dropped into France. Their job was to mark the drop zones (DZs) with green "T"s so the pilots would know where to drop their "sticks" of eighteen men per plane. There were four DZs: A, B, C, and D. Wags, Jack, and Will would be jumping into DZ D.

*****

The flight over the English Channel was relatively quiet. All Wags, Will, and Jack could hear was the dull roar of the plane's engine. Looking out over the channel, they could see the moonlight dancing on the ocean through a break in the clouds. They had more than three hours to think about their mission and what they were about to do. It was hard to believe they would be in the middle of a war in a short while. They had trained for this mission for months, but this time, it was different. It was the real thing.

As the planes approached their destination, DZ D near Angoville, all hell broke loose. Suddenly, the sky lit up with German antiaircraft fire. The noise from the enemy fire was deafening! Their plane climbed sharply to the right dodging enemy fire and trying to avoid hitting the other planes around them.

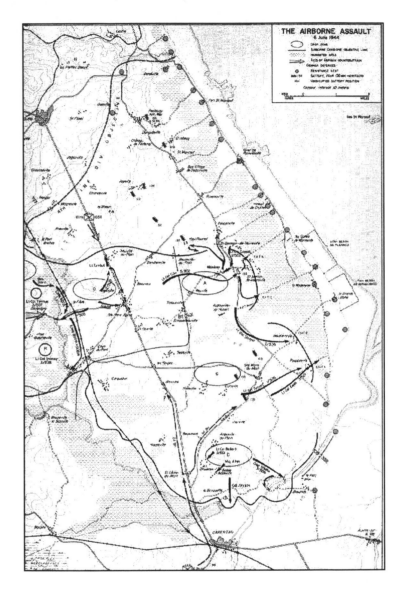

"Forget landing safely," yelled Will, "we have to get through this antiaircraft fire without getting killed! At this rate, we may not make it off the plane!"

Just then, bullets pierced the bottom of the plane.

At that point, the jumpmaster in charge of getting the paratroopers off the plane yelled to the paratroopers, "Stand up and hook up!" Wags, Will, Jack and the rest of the paratroopers tried to keep their balance when they stood up as the turbulent plane climbed steeply and banked right. It was almost impossible. They struggled as they hooked their static lines to the wire in the plane. The static line would automatically open their parachutes when they jumped out of the plane.

Jack was lucky he stood up when he did. Within seconds, bullets ripped through the seat he'd been sitting in.

"Thank God," exclaimed Jack. "I'd rather take my shot in the air than be trapped on this plane."

Anxious to get out of the plane, they pushed the men ahead of them as they had practiced in training. Once at the front of the plane, the jumpmaster gave them the signal: "Go!"

Jack jumped first, followed by Wags, then Will. As Jack jumped, he realized the plane was going a lot faster than it had been in training. His leg bag, carrying his extra pistol and ammunition was ripped off his leg by the force of the wind. He began to rethink his earlier words. *Maybe staying in the plane wasn't so bad after all,* he thought.

As he floated through the air, all Jack could see and hear were tracers whizzing past him. The realization that only one-in-six bullets were tracers terrified him. Jack still found it an awe-inspiring sight, and he just hoped he'd live to tell about it. As far as the eye could see all around him were paratroopers floating toward the French countryside. Against the backdrop of French hedgerows, it looked like they were all drifting onto a giant checkerboard.

"I knew they'd be shooting at us, but this looks like the biggest fireworks display in the world. God help the Germans if I survive this," exclaimed Jack to himself.

Just then, three bullets ripped through his parachute. "That's not good," Jack said, beginning to panic. "I hope I make it," he declared as he fell rapidly toward the French countryside, whishing past other paratroopers whose chutes remained intact. "I don't want to die—not this way…"

*****

Well, like I said, they can't kill all of us, Will thought. "I wonder if the Germans had any idea what they'd unleashed when they took over Europe and declared war on the United States?" he mumbled to himself, praying he would make it to the ground in one piece. Surprisingly, the sound of his own voice calmed him.

*****

Wags, meanwhile, did his best to pull his legs up to his chest, figuring it would make him a smaller target. *If I make it out of this alive, I swear I'll never miss church on Sunday again,* he thought, his heart racing. *This is unbelievable!*

Within a few minutes, Will and Wags had landed at opposite ends of a large field surrounded by hedgerows. Startled by a noise behind him, Wags turned quickly, pistol at the ready, to find a cow grazing. Relieved to see it was only a cow and not a German soldier, Wags took a deep breath to calm himself. He then quickly balled up his parachute and got out of his harness.

At the far corner of the next field, there was a German machine gunner firing at incoming paratroopers and planes. Wags and Will rushed to the surrounding hedgerows for cover and got out their rifles, compass, and crickets. "We've got to take out that gunner," Will said to himself, "before he takes out more of our guys."

Suddenly, there was a loud explosion near the German gunner and the machine gun fell silent. "I guess someone else had the same idea. Score one for the good guys!" said Will as he balled up his parachute.

Will walked back toward Wags, as they had been taught in training, maintaining his cover by the hedgerows. "That jump was terrifying! I can't believe we survived it," said Will, clearly shaken. "Where's Jack?"

"I have no idea," said Wags, checking his compass for direction, "but I know we have to get out of this field and start moving toward the bridges. Hopefully, we'll find him along the way."

As Wags and Will started walking, they realized just how lucky they were. They passed a number of paratroopers hit by bullets on the way down and who now lay dead on the French countryside. "Man, what a shame," Wags said soberly, shocked by the number of dead paratroopers. "They didn't even have a chance to defend themselves. I'm really starting to worry about Jack."

"Me too," said Will as he gazed around.

"These hedgerows are a lot higher and thicker than I'd expected," said Will, as he looked at the mounds of dirt six-to-twelve-feet high with thick green hedges on top. "With only one entrance to each of these fields, we're going to be sitting ducks. They provide a perfect defensive position for the Germans. Aim a machine gun at the opening and we're done. We won't even see where the gunfire is coming from," sighed Will.

"It's going to be a lot harder to fight them on this terrain. Our bullets are not going to penetrate this type of thick growth. How did the commanders miss this?" asked Wags, surprised at the lack of military intelligence.

"Probably because they only had aerial photos, which don't show the true height of the hedgerows. We all assumed they would be low and compact like the ones in England," said Will.

"I agree with you, Will. We're in for a long, hard fight," said Wags.

As they walked, they saw two paratroopers hanging dead in the trees. One of them was their colonel. Wags took a knee and removed his helmet. "May God bless their souls," Wags prayed quietly.

"Amen," said Will, slowly putting his helmet back on and discreetly wiping tears away. "He was such a great guy."

They continued to walk, silently remembering the man who, hours before, had said such an eloquent prayer:

> God Almighty! In a few hours we will be in battle with the enemy. We do not join battle afraid. We do not ask favors or indulgences but ask that, if You will, use us as Your instrument for the right and an aid in returning peace to the world. We do not know or seek what our fate will be. We only ask this, that if die we must, that we die as *men* would die; without complaining, without pleading and safe in the feeling that we have done our best for what we believed was right. Oh Lord! Protect our loved ones and be near us in the fire ahead, and with us now as we each pray to You."[iii]

"Well, at least God answered his prayer. He died as a man, fighting for what was right: Freedom," reflected Wags sadly.

Farther down the road, they saw a paratrooper struggling high in an apple tree. Wags and Will ran over to help him before the Germans found him and shot him dead. They were relieved to find that it was Jack.

"You okay?" asked Will.

"Just great!" declared Jack sarcastically. "Get me down from here."

"Wags, give me your rope," ordered Will.

"I can't," exclaimed Wags. "My leg bag got ripped off when I jumped from the plane. It was in there. I lost the flamethrower, too."

"Great!" said Will, frustrated. "Go cut some rope from one of the parachutes on the dead guys we passed. Hurry," exclaimed Will as he dropped his backpack.

"What for?" asked Wags.

"Just do it!" said Will exasperated.

Jack looked at Will perplexed. "What are you going to do?" asked Jack.

"I'm going to throw you the rope to pull you over to the branch before I cut you loose. That is, unless you want to drop fifteen feet to the ground and break your legs," laughed Will.

"Good plan," said Jack, nodding his approval. "Better hurry up though. I saw Germans approaching in the distance."

Wags came running back with the rope and gave it to Will.

"Cover us, Wags," said Will as he climbed the tree. "Jack said he saw some Germans in the distance."

Once in the tree, Will threw one end of the rope to Jack.

"Here, now wrap the rope around your waist," said Will.

Once the rope was secure around Jack's waist, Will pulled him over to the branch and cut him free from the parachute.

Will surveyed the area from the branch.

"Wags, we've got about twenty Germans heading toward us. Hide in the ditch—*now!*" yelled Will as he and Jack quickly climbed down the tree and hid behind the hedgerow.

They could hear the Germans' hobnailed boots as they rapidly approached. Luckily, they ran right by Wags, who had pressed his body against the wet dirt in the trench. When the Germans were far enough away, he climbed out of the ditch and brushed himself off.

"You guys are lifesavers," Jack said as he came out from behind the hedgerow and removed his harness.

"We're just happy to see you alive," said Wags. "A lot of guys didn't make it."

"I wasn't sure I was going to survive when the bullets ripped through my chute. That's how I ended up in the tree," Jack said, adjusting his equipment. "Where's everybody else?"

"It looks like we're scattered all over the place," said Will, frustrated. "We haven't found anyone else alive yet. I hope the 82nd Airborne fared better than we did."

Ever diligent and focused, Wags pulled out his map and looked at his compass, trying to plot a course for the foot and road bridges over the Douve River. Securing these bridges was essential to preventing the Germans from sending reinforcements to the beaches.

"Looks like we're about one mile away. Let's go," said Wags.

"We can't take the bridge by ourselves," declared Jack.

"Hopefully, we'll pick guys up along the way," said Wags. "Let's get going before the Germans find us."

As they walked toward the bridges, Will noticed a machine gunner at the corner of a field behind some hedgerows shooting at incoming planes. He looked at Jack and Wags.

"You guys ready?" he asked.

"For what?" replied Wags.

"That machine gunner isn't paying attention to what's going on behind him. He's only focused on the planes and the dropping paratroopers. If we sneak up behind him, we can take him out with a hand grenade," said Will confidently.

"Wags and I will provide cover if there are any Germans covering him," said Jack. "Will, you've got the best arm— you're in charge of the grenade."

Wags and Jack found a small opening at the bottom of the hedgerow. They struggled through the hedgerow first and got down on one knee, surveying the area for German soldiers. Will climbed through next and crawled on his stomach toward the machine gunner.

As Will got within twenty yards of the machine gun nest, he signaled to Jack and Wags. "It's just like throwing a football. Find your target, aim, and throw," whispered Will apprehensively.

Will pulled the pin to activate the grenade, stood up, and heaved the grenade into the circular machine gun nest. Suddenly, two German soldiers raced out of the nest, firing in their direction. Will quickly dove to the ground to avoid being struck by their bullets. Wags and Jack fired back, killing them instantly. The third German soldier was blown into the air when the hand grenade exploded and ignited the ammunition in the machine gun nest. The gun fell silent.

"Nice job!" exclaimed Wags, adrenaline running through his veins.

"Too little, too late," Jack said. "Look…"

Jack, Will, and Wags looked to the sky helplessly as they watched a C-47 transport plane in a fiery descent explode when it hit the ground in the next field. Wags, Jack, and Will ran toward the field to see if they could help. When they got there, nothing was left of the plane or its passengers except a fireball. Twenty men were killed in the crash.

"What a way to go," declared Will sadly.

Allied planes continued dropping troops as they walked away, heading toward the bridges. The gunfire was deafening. Suddenly, they saw movement in the hedgerows. They immediately sought cover, fearing the movement might be German soldiers. Jack used his cricket clicker. There was no response. He tried again. Finally, after what seemed like a lifetime, He got the cricket clicker response.

"Thunder," whispered Jack.

"Lightening," answered BJ.

Coming out from behind the hedgerow were four American soldiers, soaking wet.

"I'm Jack. This is Wags and Will. We're with the 101st. How about you guys?" Jack asked, relieved to have found more paratroopers.

"I'm BJ. This is Joe. We're with the 82nd Airborne. Raf and Mike are 101st."

"Well, so much for hoping the 82nd had better luck than we did," said Will.

"Why are you guys so wet?" Wags asked.

"We landed in the flooded areas. Except for the fact that Joe is such a good swimmer, he would be dead right now," said John. "The rest of us landed in waist-deep water. Joe landed in water over his head and had to cut off his equipment so he could swim to shallow water. He grabbed a rifle off a dead soldier."

"We're headed for the bridges over the Douve River," indicated Wags as he pulled out his map. "I figure we're roughly three-quarters of a mile away about now."

"How far do you think we are from Sainte-Mère-Église?" asked Joe. "That's our objective."

"About ten miles to the northeast," Wags said.

"We should stay together," said BJ. "We'll be safer in numbers. Besides, we'd never make it there in time, and it's starting to get light. We're going to lose our cover."

Just then, the bombardment of the shorelines began. They looked at each other. The second wave of the invasion was beginning. The ground shook with every explosion.

"Some of those bombs are coming awfully close. I thought they were supposed to be hitting the shoreline, not us!" said Raf, nervous at the prospect of being killed by American bombs.

"Well, it's not like the planes can drop the bombs precisely. Let's just hope we don't become victims of friendly fire," said Mike.

"Oh great," said Jack, shaking his head. "Like we don't have enough to worry about."

"C'mon. We have to get moving. Securing those bridges is essential to preventing a counterattack by the Germans," declared Will. "And keep an eye out for the equipment bundles that were dropped from the planes—something tells me we're going to need them."

CHAPTER FIVE

Heading to Omaha Beach

While Wags, Jack, Will, and the others were making their way to the Douve River bridges to prevent a German counterattack on the landing forces, Christopher, Kevin, and Brian—along with thousands of other soldiers—had boarded their assigned LCVP (landing craft, vehicle and personnel). There were more than four thousand landing boats of various sizes.[iv] The LCVP, nicknamed the "Higgins boat" after its designer, was a large boat (thirty-six-feet long and more than ten-and-one-half-feet wide) with a square bow that doubled as a ramp. It could carry either thirty-six men or one jeep and twelve men. Once ashore, it could drop off soldiers in seconds and return to the troop transports to pick up more men. The LCVPs landed on the beaches in waves.

Christopher, Kevin, Brian, and thirty-three other soldiers climbed down the nets on the sides of the transport ship to board the LCVP bouncing around on the choppy water. Once aboard, it took everything they had not to throw up. The dinner at the pub had been only a few weeks earlier, but it seemed like a lifetime ago. Kevin could not help but worry about his long-time friends Wags and Will.

"I wonder how the 101st Airborne is doing right now?" Kevin said.

Instinctively, Christopher looked at Kevin and said, "Wags and Will are just fine."

"I hope so," said Kevin.

Christopher, Kevin, and Brian had to travel twelve miles through choppy water to land on Omaha Beach with the larger Navy ships following behind as they made their approach. The LCVP was tossed around by the large channel swells, and when some of the other soldiers onboard began throwing up from seasickness, Christopher looked at Kevin and said, "It's going to be a looong trip!"

As they traveled toward Omaha Beach they waited for the pre-invasion air bombardment to begin, but everything was silent. The sun was just beginning to rise when, suddenly, they heard bombs exploding. Unfortunately, the bombs were landing too far inland. The beaches were clear, and there was no evidence of any air support where the Allied Forces were going to land. Soon, the Navy battleships, cruisers, and destroyers began firing on the coastline.

Kevin looked excitedly at Christopher and Brian and declared, "It's on now!"

Christopher, realizing the air bombardment was critical to the success of the invasion, grew concerned. Just then, a large wave rocked their LCVP, throwing them around the landing craft.

"What was that from?" yelled Brian, looking around the landing craft.

"Be prepared," said Christopher. "Every time a battle-ship or destroyer fires their guns, it's going to cause waves like that." Just then, the sea spray came over the sides of the LCVP, drenching them with the cold water from the English Channel.

"Great," replied Brian, trying desperately not to throw up. "Now I'm not only sick, but I'm freezing, too."

Kevin laughed. "This is unbelievable! I've never seen anything like it. This should be a cakewalk."

Christopher knew better. The absence of an air attack on the beaches would be devastating to the landing troops. They were supposed to take out the German defenses on the beach. If there were no pre-invasion bombings, the German forces would be devastating to the ground effort.

When the men began to land on Omaha Beach, the ships stopped firing for fear of hitting them. After three hours of bouncing around on the sea, it became very clear to those waiting to go ashore that the invasion was not go-ing as planned.

The screaming noise of incoming German shells and the "ack-ack-ack" of the machine guns above the beach was deafening. The putrid smell of burning oil and con-stant sounds of ammunition exploding was terrifying. When it came time for Christopher, Kevin, and Brian's LCVP to land on the beach, Christopher looked over at Kevin and Brian. Gone was the confidence Kevin had exuded when the naval barrage began—it had now been replaced with fear. *They seem to have aged ten years in the last few minutes*, thought Christopher. Much to their horror, the LCVP next to them was hit by a German shell, killing everyone on board. Then, the LCVP behind them exploded after hitting a mine.

Suddenly, the boatswain piloting their landing craft screamed over the noise of the guns and explosions, "Get ready! We're going in!" The ship surged toward the beach. In an instant, the heavy metal ramp dropped quickly, exposing all the men aboard to German gunfire. The men in front of Christopher, Kevin, and Brian were shot by German machine gunners before they could even get off the ramp.

Christopher screamed, "Get over the side *now!*"

Kevin and Brian quickly followed him over the five-foot-high side of the Higgins boat. Once in the cold water, Brian sank from the weight of his backpack. Christopher scooped Brian up and pulled him to safety just as he was reaching to inflate his Mae West life preserver. Kevin was nowhere to be found.

Brian, gasping for air, looked around, startled and yelled, "Thanks!"

Brian began screaming for Kevin, when he suddenly appeared behind Brian. "I'm here, Bri," Kevin said. "I was looking for you."

"Christopher pulled me up just in time," declared Brian.

"It's a good thing you told us to jump over the side," said Brian, "or we'd be dead!"

As Christopher surveyed the bloody scene around him, he saw the beach filled with burning vehicles and dead and wounded soldiers. More dead soldiers were floating in the water. The sounds of gunfire and bombs, and the screams of the wounded and dying were unrelenting. The smell around them was revolting. *Oh my God, we've arrived in hell,* thought Christopher.

Wading in the cold water, the Fighting Hawks dodged bullets on their way to the gray-steel Czech hedgehog obstacle.

"I guess they know we're here," said Christopher, smiling, hoping to calm Kevin and Brian's fear. "We need a plan."

Behind the obstacle, Christopher, Kevin, and Brian surveyed the beach. They had to run across a sandy area the length of three football fields to get to the protection of the seawall. There were more than a thousand dead and wounded American soldiers up and down the beach. Many of them were missing legs and arms. Some of them had been cut in half by machine-gun fire. The water was red from their blood. Meanwhile, the Germans continued their unending firing at the soldiers still trying to get across the beach.

To make matters worse, the Germans had blown up all the vehicles and tanks that had made it ashore. The beach was littered with burning tanks, jeeps, and artillery that prevented other boats from coming ashore. It looked like an obstacle course.

"I'm going to puke" said Kevin, gagging.

"Save it 'til later! We don't have time for that right now," said Christopher sternly, surveying the bluff with his binoculars.

The three of them watched as soldier after soldier was cut down by the barrage of gunfire coming from the German machine gunners on the bluff.

"How in God's name are we going to get across the beach?" asked Kevin.

"Drop your backpacks!" yelled Christopher loudly.

"What? Our supplies are in it," screamed Brian over the gunfire.

"It's also seventy pounds," replied Kevin, clearly frustrated and angry at the scene ahead of them. "He's right. We'll grab another one when we get to the seawall. Dodging bullets with that pack is going to get us killed."

Brian, regaining his composure, looked over at Kevin. The fear in his face was evident. *Well, at least I'm not the only one scared to death*, he thought. However, when he looked at

Christopher, it was clear that he was evaluating the situation ahead of them. Somehow, he didn't seem afraid.

Christopher turned to Kevin and Brian. "There're dozens of machine guns placed in pillboxes and trenches above us," pointing to the bluff. "The bigger guns are near the entrances to the draws. As best as I can tell, they've got every inch of this beach covered with cross-firing weapons."

"How are we going to get across the beach?" screamed Kevin ducking behind the obstacle.

"We've got to get away from groups of soldiers running up together. Because of the tides and currents, we're landing in bunches, and the Germans are focusing their fire on them," Christopher yelled back.

Kevin and Brian looked around the beach nearest to them.

"We need to get over to the next obstacle on our left. It's only twenty-five yards away, and there are less men over there. It's about thirty yards closer to the beach, too. Less distance to the seawall," yelled Kevin over the gunfire.

Christopher and Brian looked to see where it was. "Good job, Kev. Now you're thinking like a soldier," said Christopher. "Stay low and don't bunch up. I'm first, Brian's next, and then you."

Christopher got down in the water so only his head was exposed, crawling on the sandy bottom. *It was much more fun at the Jersey shore when I wasn't being shot at*, thought Christopher. *I hope I live to do that again someday.*

Brian and Kevin followed his lead. Waiting until Christopher was twenty-five feet ahead of him, Brian got down in the water and crab-crawled his way over to the next obstacle. As he did so, he suddenly felt a searing pain in his arm. *Damn! I'm hit*, thought Brian, grabbing his arm.

Kevin, worried, watched as Brian clutched his arm and made his way to Christopher. Suddenly, it was his turn to go.

This current is really strong. No wonder we're all landing off course, thought Kevin as he fought the current to get over to Christopher and Brian behind the next obstacle.

When Kevin got there, he found Christopher looking at Brian's arm. "Nothing but a flesh wound, Brian," said Christopher, relieved.

"Told you I was okay," declared Brian, not wanting to be treated like a baby.

"Now what?" asked Kevin.

"Remember to run in a zigzag pattern and stay low. Use the burning tanks for cover when you can," advised Christopher.

"Go!" screamed Brian, fear engulfing him.

The three made a mad dash for the seawall, dodging bullets along the way. Although running as fast as they could, the weight of their waterlogged uniforms slowed them down significantly. As they got close, Kevin slipped on the slippery rock shingle and hit the ground. Brian turned to help him.

"Keep going," screamed Kevin, gunfire all around him.

"No! I'm not leaving you!" Brian yelled, grabbing Kevin's collar and dragging him to his feet.

Seconds later, machine gunfire strafed where Kevin had fallen. "That was close. Thanks Bri," screamed Kevin.

Christopher made it to the seawall first, followed by Kevin and Brian. When they got there, they realized there was nowhere to go. Barbed wire blocked the exits. They were trapped, along with other soldiers who had been lucky enough to make it that far. The tanks that were supposed to clear the way were burning on the beach.

Finding equipment that had been dropped near the seawall, they took rifles, grenades, bangalore torpedoes, and whatever else they could get their hands on, realizing that they were taking supplies from dead American soldiers.

While Christopher searched for a way off the beach, Kevin and Brian took in the scene around them. They watched as the medics ran from injured soldier to injured soldier trying to help them. Some of the men bled from the head, and others had lost hands, arms, or feet. Farther down the beach, they saw the chaplains administering last rites to the dead and dying soldiers.

"I can't believe those guys. They're risking their own lives to help others," said Kevin to Brian.

"How are they doing that? I'm terrified! All I want to do is get off this beach," said Brian.

Kevin looked at Brian. "They're the best example of being a 'Man for Others' I've ever seen," said Kevin.

"Me too!" said Brian.

In the meantime, Christopher had an idea. He yelled to Brian, "You have any bangalore torpedoes?"

"Yeah, why?" asked Brian.

"Hand me one," yelled Christopher over the gunfire.

"What are you going to do with it?" Kevin asked.

"Blow a hole in the barbed wire trapping us on the beach," yelled Christopher over the gunfire. "Take cover!" Christopher screamed seconds before the torpedo exploded.

When they looked up again, there was a large hole in the barbed wire, giving the trapped soldiers a path off the beach. "C'mon guys! Let's go!" yelled Christopher.

As Christopher advanced past the seawall, going over the shingle and through the booby-trapped swamp, Brian helped guide him past the landmines. Kevin and the other soldiers provided cover fire as best as they could.

"How're you doing this?" asked Christopher as they headed up the draw through the minefield.

"It's easy," said Brian. "Look closely, you'll see a trail the Germans use to get up and down the beach. You just have to be careful to double-check for tripwires."

"Well, keep your eyes open then," yelled Christopher. He was marking the way with white tape so those behind him could find a safe path through the marshy minefield on the bluff. Brian stayed right behind him, helping guide the way. Christopher trusted Brian's instincts.

As they made their way up the bluff, Kevin noticed gunfire coming from a well-camouflaged German machine gun up the hill in a deep, narrow trench to his right. They were firing in the opposite direction at the landing troops on the beach.

"Cover me," Kevin told the soldiers behind him. *Here goes nothing*, he thought, his heart racing as he snuck up behind the machine gunner. He pulled the pin on the grenade and lobbed it into the trench from ten yards away.

Suddenly, he heard the Germans screaming, trying to get out of the trench. Then, the grenade exploded and they went quiet. Kevin went over the top of the trench firing his gun to make sure all the Germans were dead.

Once atop the bluff, Christopher, Kevin, and Brian—along with other soldiers who had been trapped on the beach—entered the lightly defended town of Vierville. After that, Christopher headed back toward the beach.

Brian looked at Christopher and asked, "Where are you going?"

Christopher replied, "We're going to flank the machine gunners over the beach and take them out."

Kevin turned to Christopher and yelled, "What are you? Crazy?"

Christopher looked at Kevin, shook his head, and said, "Did you see all those men shot to pieces on the beach? Who the hell do you think is doing that? Germans! Except for Brian's contingency plan, that could have been us. We've got to go back and help the other guys coming in. If we circle behind the German emplacements and machine gunners in the trenches, we can take some of them out and save lives."

"Good point," Kevin said, embarrassed. "I just thought our orders were to continue to move inland."

"They were," declared Christopher. "But it was also supposed to be a cakewalk onto the beach. Time to improvise again."

Brian, in the meantime, had rounded up other soldiers to go with them. "Let's go," he yelled. "We're wasting valuable time."

As they doubled back toward the beach, it became clear that Christopher's strategy would work. They were now behind the Germans. They divided the soldiers into groups to ambush the German soldiers in their well-concealed cement-and-steel machine-gun emplacements and trenches. The Germans had no idea they were approaching.

Kevin rapidly approached an emplacement from behind, grenade in hand.

"Cover me," he told Brian.

Kevin pulled the pin to the grenade, snuck up beside the emplacement and tossed the grenade inside. Again, he heard the Germans moving around and screaming inside. Kevin waited for the explosion. After it exploded, Brian circled to the front of the emplacement and fired his rifle into the opening to make sure everyone was dead.

Following the trenches, Brian found another gun emplacement. "I've got this one," Brian said. Crawling on his stomach, he slowly approached the gun emplacement.

With the other soldiers providing cover, he reached up to the front of the emplacement and threw in a phosphorous grenade that burns the skin. Suddenly, the backdoor of the emplacement opened, and German soldiers ran out screaming. The soldiers covering Brian shot them on the spot.

"Nice job," yelled Brian. "Now, we're getting somewhere!"

While Kevin and Brian moved in on the emplacements, Christopher and some of the other soldiers advanced ahead of them. They found a series of trenches leading from machine gun to machine gun. The trenches were very narrow and deep. Christopher took the lead. As he came to each sharp corner, he would carefully, but quickly, look ahead to make sure it was safe to proceed.

"Let's go," declared Christopher, waving the men forward. "Have your grenades and rifles ready."

As Christopher fought his way through the trenches, he encountered other soldiers who had come up from the beach by a different route.

"How did you get here?" asked Christopher, surprised to see them.

"We came up the bluff on the east side. We met a lot resistance, but some of us were able to advance," declared Mark.

Together, the soldiers fought through the trenches to eliminate the German resistance. They killed more than ninety German soldiers using grenades and rifles. By taking out many of the German emplacements near the Vierville draw, they provided a second escape route for soldiers stranded on the beach. Equally important, they stopped or distracted the Germans from shooting at the landing parties on the beach.

As the Fighting Hawks looked out over Omaha Beach, they were both horrified and awestruck. The carnage on the beach was indescribable. There were burning tanks and vehicles. The mangled bodies of more than a thousand American soldiers lay dead on the beach or floated in the bloody ocean water. They watched as more soldiers scrambled toward the seawall, dodging bullets along the way or being killed in their tracks.

Looking out over the ocean, they saw boats and landing craft as far as the eye could see, all waiting for their turn to disembark on the beach.

"It's like leading lambs to the slaughter," declared Christopher, looking like he wanted to strangle someone. "I knew the Nazi's were evil, but I never expected this."

Kevin looked away. One year earlier, he and Will had graduated from St. Peter's Prep, vowing to be "Men for Others." *How is this happening?* he thought. *They taught us at Prep to help each other, not kill each other.*

Suddenly, Kevin felt an anger rise in him unlike any he had ever known. Those men lying on the beach were fathers, sons, husbands, and brothers who were never going to see their families again. "C'mon, we've got to help those guys!" he yelled.

"Wait!" Brian said, putting out his hand to stop him. "Look!"

Christopher, Kevin, and the rest of the soldiers looked out over the ocean. Suddenly, they saw the one of the destroyers heading toward the beach. It was the USS *McCook*. Against strict orders not to fire once the landing began, the destroyer fired the ship's five-inch guns at the German emplacements above the beach. Within minutes, every American destroyer followed their lead, firing at the numerous German gun emplacements above the beach.

"We've got to get out of here *now*," screamed Christopher. "If one of those shells misses, we're dead meat. They'll take care of the rest. Move it!"

The Fighting Hawks raced back to the village of Vierville to link up with the hundreds of soldiers who had managed to get off the beach.

When they got back, Christopher and Kevin sat down under a tree to rest while the commanders decided the next course of action. Brian was over by a truck talking with some of the other soldiers.

"How do you do it?" Kevin asked, thinking about what he had just witnessed on the beach.

"What?" asked Christopher softly.

"Stay so calm and focused after seeing what we just saw?" said Kevin, clearly shaken.

"You get used to it," answered Christopher, calmly eating his K ration.

"How? I don't think I'll ever get used to this," replied Kevin.

"I felt the same way after my first time," Christopher said. "I watched my best friend gunned down right before my eyes. It should have been me, but he jumped in front of me," said Christopher. "It took a lot of soul searching to figure out why I lived and he died."

"What did you come up with?" asked Kevin.

"It's simple really. My dad always said there's an invisible date on your forehead. That's the day you're going to die. You just don't know it," said Christopher, shrugging his shoulders.

He went on, "Over here, I call it the 'War God'. If the War God has your number, there's nothing you can do about it. He'll take you when it's your time to go, so there's no point in worrying about it because you can't change it. You do your best and pray that he doesn't have your number."

"What if he does?" Kevin asked.

"I guess you'll be guarding the streets of heaven with all the other soldiers who have gone before us, watching over the rest of us," said Christopher calmly, taking another bite. "Let me ask you something. What is this 'Man for Others' thing you keep talking about?"

"When we were at Prep, the Jesuit priests constantly instilled in us the importance of doing things for others. You know, putting other people ahead of yourself," replied Kevin. "Why?"

"Well, just for the record, every man here is a 'Man for Others,'" replied Christopher.

Kevin looked perplexed.

"Kev, we're here on foreign soil for one reason and one reason only: Freedom. We're here to free the people of Europe from Hitler's domination and brutality. The men fighting in the Pacific are there to free those people from Japan's domination and brutality. And we're all fighting to keep our families free and safe at home," said Christopher. "When we defeat Hitler, the deaths of all these men will not be in vain.'

"Makes sense," said Kevin with a smile. "Thanks."

"No problem. What about Brian? Is he going to be okay?" asked Christopher.

"I don't know," answered Kevin. "He keeps everything in. He doesn't talk about his feelings much, you know?"

"I've noticed that. We'll have to keep an eye on him then," said Christopher. "What we see and do here takes its toll on everybody."

Just then, they got the orders to move out.

CHAPTER SIX

Securing the Bridges[v]

In the meantime, Wags, Will, Jack, and the others walked towards the Douve Bridges. They were very quiet, except for Jack who would use his cricket clicker occasionally.

"Would you stop that?" whispered Will.

"How else are we going to find our 'stick'?" asked Jack. "I don't really feel like fighting this war by ourselves."

"Look, if we just head toward our objective, we'll find more people," stated Wags.

As they walked, Jack continued to click his cricket clicker. Slowly, he began to hear a response. Jack would whisper, "thunder." If the person on the other end of the cricket clicker was an American, they would respond, "lightning."

By 6:00 a.m., they had found another fifteen paratroopers, some from the 101st and others from the 82nd airborne. Three of them were injured. Wags helped the injured soldiers to the aid station set up by some of the other paratroopers at a local farm. After they dropped off the wounded, they headed to the bridges. Along the way, Wags located a German communications line.

"You have any explosives?" Wags asked Will.

"How much do you need?" said Will.

"Two-and-a-half pounds should be enough. We just have to destroy this communications line," stated Wags.

Jack and the other soldiers were looking out for Germans. "Hurry up, you guys," urged Jack. "We're out in the open here."

Will handed Wags the explosives and a fuse to detonate it. Wags quickly placed the explosives and the fuse at the base of the communications lines.

"Take cover!" yelled Wags as he lit the fuse.

They ducked down in a nearby ditch just as the explosion went off, covering them with dirt.

"That was close," declared Jack. "What's next?"

"We've got to secure the foot and road bridges over the Douve River," stated Will.

"We going to blow them up?" asked Wags.

"No," said Will, "we need to secure them so the guys landing at Utah and Omaha Beaches can move inland and the Germans can't launch a counterattack over them."

The tall, thick hedgerows provided great cover as they headed toward the bridges. Just then, Jack clicked his cricket clicker again. Will looked at him.

"Nothing like drawing attention to us," declared Will sarcastically.

"The more the merrier," stated Jack with a big grin.

As they made their way to the bridges, they realized the Germans were defending them with machine guns. They couldn't tell how many Germans were there.

"Now what?" asked Jack, crouching behind the brush near the river.

Will pulled out his binoculars and evaluated the situation. On the other side of the bridge, the terrain was hilly and elevated. There were several machine gun emplacements, and the Germans had the tactical advantage of being able to look down and see the movements of the Allied paratroopers. Fortunately, on their side of the bridge, there were two dykes that acted as a flood barrier for the Douve River. One dyke was about ten feet high, the other a little lower. The lower dyke was two hundred yards closer to the river. Both dykes provided excellent cover for the Allied soldiers. Unfortunately, the Germans had the same dykes to hide in on the other side. It was a perfect spot for an ambush.

"We have to capture those guns. It's not going to be easy," said Will tentatively. "We've got to get some guys across the bridge, and as best as I can tell, the only way to do it is with a head-on assault. We can provide cover for them from this side, but it's going to be difficult and dangerous."

BJ, Joe, and a few other soldiers they had picked up along the way from the 82nd Airborne stepped up. "We can do it!" they volunteered.

While Will set up the covering fire positions, BJ looked at Joe and the others. Drawing a map in the dirt, BJ showed the group how they were going to fan out once they got across the bridge.

"Guys, I'll take the lead position going across the bridge. Stay at least five feet apart and walk on opposite sides. We don't want to bunch up and make an easy target for the Germans. Most important, stay low," ordered BJ emphatically.

"Ready?" asked Will.

"As ready as we are ever going to be," BJ declared, pulling his submachine gun from his shoulder, ready to fire if necessary.

Laying low on the dyke, ready to provide covering fire, Wags, Jack, Will and the remaining soldiers watched as the men advanced across the flat wooden bridge, all the while looking for any signs of life from the Germans. BJ slowly led the group across the bridge, scanning the hill ahead for any sign of trouble. Joe and the others followed behind, carefully observing the scene ahead of them.

As BJ neared the other side of the river, he jumped over the side of the bridge onto the mud below, and the others followed. Once on the riverbed, they were beneath the berm of a dyke. Cautiously, they began separating and moving upstream. A German soldier suddenly appeared on the top of the dyke and began firing at them. Joe took a bullet in the upper chest and dropped to the ground. BJ turned, saw the German soldier standing over Joe, and shot him with his submachine gun.

"Damn!" screamed Jack, firing toward the berm.

As the other soldiers ran back to help Joe, Will began firing his mortar rounds over the river at the Germans to prevent a large counterattack. BJ and the rest of the men were out in the open and easy targets.

"Joe, use this!" yelled BJ, handing him a wooden plank left over from the bridge construction.

"For what?" asked Joe, trying to apply pressure to his wound.

"Slide it between the bridge supports under the wooden planks and climb across. The bridge will give you cover," yelled BJ, as he shot at the Germans above him.

While Jack, Wags, Will, and the others engaged in a firefight with the Germans, providing cover for BJ and the other men on the bridge, Joe desperately tried to get back to safety. It was a painfully slow process as he placed the board, climbed across it, moved it between the next bridge support, and then repeated the process. When he finally got back to the Allied side, he could not get up the steep, damp berm.

"Wags, cover me! I've got to help Joe," hollered Jack, as he went over the higher berm to get Joe.

Wags provided covering fire for Jack.

"Grab this," yelled Jack, as he threw a rope over to Joe.

"Thanks," hollered Joe over the gunfire.

Weak from blood loss, Joe gathered his strength and grabbed the rope. Jack and several other soldiers pulled him to safety over the berm and administered first aid.

The Germans kept lobbing mortar shells all around them. BJ and the others slowly retreated back across the river under the protective fire from Wags, Will, Jack, and the other Allied Forces troops with them. They dug in to prevent the Germans from crossing the bridge and advancing toward the beaches. They found themselves in a standoff.

"We've got to get word to headquarters that we're meeting resistance and we need more fire power," said Will. "Does *anybody* have a working radio?"

"I already checked, and we don't," answered Wags. "I sent two of the guys from the 82nd to notify HQ."

Will looked at Wags and Jack.

"We've got to rig this bridge with explosives just in case we can't hold them," declared Will. "They've got to be mobilizing their forces by now."

"Some guys from the Airborne Engineers showed up a little while ago," stated Jack. "You want me to find them?"

"Yeah," said Wags. "Send them over."

Later, under cover of nightfall, the Airborne Engineers rigged the bridge with explosives in case it needed to be blown up to prevent a German counterattack.

As Wags, Jack and Will watched the engineers rig the bridge from their foxhole, Will looked at Wags.

"You think the guys from the 82nd got to HQ?" asked Will.

"I don't know. It really depends on how successful the other paratroopers were in securing their objectives," said Wags.

"It also depends on whether the guys at HQ have a working radio," declared Jack sarcastically. "What a mess."

"Well, at least we reached our objective," said Wags proudly.

They continued guarding the bridges overnight and into the next day as the men from the beaches began moving inland. At noon, they heard Allied planes approaching. Relieved to see the Allies still had control of the air, they waved at the planes. Suddenly, they saw bombs drop from the bellies of the planes.

"Duck!" screamed Will, diving into the foxhole on top of Jack.

"Guess they don't know we're here!" yelled Jack. "Maybe those guys never made it to HQ yesterday."

Once the explosions subsided, Jack, Wags, and Will peered over the side of the foxhole at the destroyed bridges. Their hearts sank. The bridges they had fought so hard to defend were destroyed by their own troops.

Will stood up, and looked around at the soldiers that had been defending the bridge.

"That was close. Anybody hurt?" yelled Will.

"Nah, we're okay," the soldiers replied.

"What now?" asked Wags, turning to Will.

"We stay put until we get more men. The Germans can still cross the river, even without a bridge," declared Will.

CHAPTER SEVEN

Back to Class: Analyzing the Battle

"Cosgrove!" the mild mannered Sgt. Carney screamed at the top of his lungs.

"Sir, yes sir," replied a startled Christopher, jumping to attention.

"Since you've spent this entire class ignoring me, perhaps you would like to recap what the class learned today," Sgt. Carney challenged, sure that Cosgrove would be on latrine duty for the next week.

"Start with the successes and failures of the D-Day invasion and what factors influenced those successes and failures."

"Sir, yes sir," shouted Christopher.

"There were many factors that contributed to the success of the invasion. The first factor was the timing of the invasion, and in many ways, that was just luck. The weatherman General Eisenhower relied on to predict the weather anticipated a lull in the storm that started on June 5, 1944. That storm delayed the invasion by one day. The German weatherman did not predict the lull. As a result, Field Marshall Rommel, who was in charge of the German troops at Normandy, decided to go home to Germany for his wife's birthday. Rommel did not believe the Allied Forces would launch an invasion due to the poor weather conditions. He thought the Allies would wait for four to five days of predicted good weather and appropriate tide conditions. The next time that would happen would be about two weeks later. Additionally, other German commanders were on a map exercise in Renes. Finally, Hitler was sleeping at the time of the invasion. He was the only one who could order the deadly Panzer tanks into action. Since Hitler waited ten hours to engage the Panzers, the Allies were able to get a foothold in the region," stated Christopher.

"Go on," said Sgt. Carney intrigued.

"Because the German soldiers were trained to act only on orders, they did not know how to improvise. Even if they knew how to improvise, they would not act without orders from their superiors," indicated Christopher.

"The Allied Forces, on the other hand, were great at improvising. While they still followed the chain of command, they were not afraid to make their own decisions and move forward. The ability to analyze and react was essential to the Allied Forces given the numerous missteps on D-Day," said Christopher.

Impressed, Sgt. Carney told Christopher, "Please continue."

Christopher went on. "The Germans' delayed reaction and confused response gave the Allied paratroopers time to destroy many communications lines. The German troops' inability to communicate with their commanders from the front lines and their reliance on orders from superiors delayed their reaction to the invasion even further.

"Another factor contributing to the success of the D-Day invasion was Hitler's belief that the invasion at Normandy was a diversionary tactic. As a result of false information provided to Hitler by captured Nazi spies, he held back two hundred fifty thousand troops as well as most of his Panzer tanks because he believed the 'real attack' would come at Pas-de-Calais in northern France. Hitler held these forces back until June 16, 1944, long after the Allied Forces had developed a stronghold in France," declared Christopher.

"Name one of the missteps of the Allied Forces," said Sgt. Carney.

"General Eisenhower's decision to invade on June 6, 1944, had its downside for the Allied Forces as well," said Christopher. "Because the weather was overcast with low clouds, many of the Army's B-17 bombers dropped their bombs from twenty thousand feet. Because they were flying above the clouds, they couldn't see their targets. Many of the bombs that should have landed on targets at the Normandy Beaches actually landed two to three miles inland, causing unintended deaths to the paratroopers and French civilians or the bombs were brought back to England. Less than half the B-17s dropped their bombs. The B-24s also failed to provide the air support needed at Omaha, Sword, and Gold Beaches, making the landings much more difficult for the troops."

Christopher continued: "The B-26 pilots, on the other hand, were flying below the cloud line. They were amazed by the sight of the thousands of landing craft as well as remaining support ships behind them. They watched as the Navy ships fired on the coastline. However, since their objective was Utah Beach, they did not drop any bombs on Omaha Beach. As a result of their bombing runs, the landings at Utah Beach were much safer. General Eisenhower had counted on the success of the air bombardment to clear the way for the men landing on the beaches. Unfortunately, it didn't work that way," stated Christopher, shaking his head slowly.

"Why not?" asked Sgt. Carney.

"As I said, the B-17s couldn't see their targets. The B-24s were afraid they were going to hit the incoming invasion forces due to the inaccuracies of the bombs. Unlike the Navy's ability to accurately place bombs at a specified location, the bombs dropped from the Allied planes could not be controlled. Making matters worse, the Germans had done a spectacular job of building and camouflaging the pillboxes that contained the machine guns focused on the beach. They were heavily fortified with concrete and steel rods making them almost impossible to destroy," indicated Christopher.

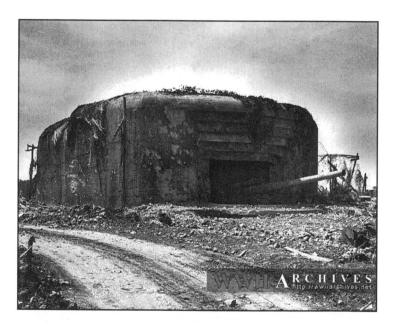

"If that was the case," asked Sgt. Carney, "how did the infantry finally get off of the beaches?"

"Well," said Christopher, "that would be the second and equally important factor contributing to the success of the Allied invasion on D-Day."

"The Navy's performance was exceptional, especially the destroyers. In many ways, it was the decision of the lieutenants, lieutenant commanders, and captains on the destroyers to violate their original orders not to fire on the coastline when the invasion forces were landing on the beaches. After approximately three hours of watching the Allied Forces being blown apart as they landed, these men took it upon themselves—again, against orders—to begin firing above the troops on the shoreline at the heavily camouflaged pillboxes on Omaha Beach. Their decision saved the lives of countless men and gave the infantry the ability to get off the beach," declared Christopher. "That was another example of the Allied Forces ability to improvise and act, in this case, in direct contravention to their orders, because based on their observations, the invasion plan was failing."

"Finally, Admiral Bryant ordered all of the destroyers to open fire on the shoreline. As a result, the destroyers sailed up and down Omaha Beach, firing every gun they had," added Christopher.

"What happened on the other beaches?" asked Sgt. Carney.

"The British landings at Gold and Sword Beaches were comparatively easy. However, the Canadians, who landed at Juno Beach between Gold and Sword, had a very difficult time," stated Christopher.

"Why was that?" asked Sgt. Carney.

"Well," replied Christopher, "the Canadians arrived about thirty minutes late, just as the tide was beginning to rise. As a result, many of the landing craft at Juno Beach were destroyed by underwater mines and German obstacles. All tolled, approximately one thousand men were lost at Juno Beach during the invasion."

"What happened at Utah Beach?" questioned Sgt. Carney.

"Luck was on the side of the troops landing at Utah Beach," declared Christopher. "The naval bombardment was much more successful in hitting the gun emplacements. The coastal bombing by the planes was more accurate as well. Those successes, combined with the fact that the troops landed approximately two-thirds of a mile south of their designated landing zone—an area not well defended by the Germans—made for a successful landing. Fewer than two hundred men lost their lives at Utah Beach," indicated Christopher happily.

"Good," declared Sgt. Carney. "There was one other factor that played into the successful landing at Utah Beach. What was it?"

"The successes of the 101st Airborne in securing Pouppeville, a small inland town," said Christopher proudly. "By the end of D-Day at Utah beach, the Americans were able to bring twenty-three thousand five hundred troops and seventeen hundred tanks, trucks, and other machinery ashore, as well as set up their headquarters."

"What about the rest of the paratroopers? How did the air invasion go?" questioned Sgt. Carney.

"Quite honestly, sir, it was a mess," declared Christopher.

"Really? Why?" asked Sgt. Carney.

"Actually, there are two reasons. Many of the planes flew into thick clouds. They separated and lost their bearings, dropping their paratroopers off target. Also, as the planes flew over France, the Germans fired on them with countless antiaircraft guns. As the planes tried to avoid the barrage of gunfire and each other, many of the troops were dropped too low. Those men died on impact because their parachutes never opened. Others were dropped too high, which left them as sitting ducks for the machine gunners and placed them far from their intended drop zone. Still others landed in flooded fields or the English Channel and drowned because they were so heavily weighed down by their equipment. Also, some paratroopers landed in the middle of heavily fortified areas. They were immediately taken prisoner or killed. Finally, many of the planes were going too fast when they dropped their men, and the paratroopers lost their equipment when they jumped due to the speed."

Christopher continued, "A major problem experienced by almost all the paratroopers was the inability to communicate with other units. Many units lost their radios during the jump. Their commanders assumed that the troops had been killed or captured, or were unable to meet their objectives, even though they had. As a result, bridges were destroyed that had already been secured, and troops were killed by friendly fire from the air as they moved toward their objectives."

"Why, then, does history indicate that the paratroopers were essential to the success of the invasion?" questioned Sgt. Carney.

"Despite all of the mishaps, the massive air invasion confused the Germans. They had no clear idea of how many paratroopers there were or where they were. The Allied Forces even dropped dummy paratroopers with tape recorders in them to confuse the Germans. The dummy paratroopers kept potential advancing German forces distracted trying to capture the dummies," declared Christopher.

"The Allied paratroopers did their best to find each other using their cricket clickers. While some paratroopers wandered alone for days, others were able to find each other and band together in small groups, gathering more men as they headed toward their objectives."

"What if they had different objectives?" asked Sgt. Carney.

"It depended on the circumstances. In some cases, troops were dropped so far from their objectives that they modified their objectives and fought with the soldiers they encountered along the way. It was not uncommon for members of the 101st Airborne and the 82nd Airborne to fight together for the first few days. Once their objectives were met, they moved on to reunite with their units. Others moved toward their objectives immediately, leaving the remaining paratroopers to find other members of their unit to fight with," indicated Christopher.

"You said before that the paratroopers helped ensure the success of the Utah Beach landing. How did that happen?" inquired Sgt. Carney.

"Well, not all the paratroopers were dropped off target. Some of the 'sticks' actually landed close to their drop zone and were able to meet their D-Day objectives, like securing Pouppeville. Some members of the 101st Airborne were in the town as troops that had landed at Utah Beach came up the causeways. They provided cover fire to protect the invading forces against the small force of Germans defending that area of the beach," stated Christopher.

He went on, "By the end of the day, the number of Germans surrendering to the Americans at Utah Beach became a logistical problem. They had nowhere to put them."

"Why did they have so many Germans surrendering?" questioned Sgt. Carney.

"Except for Omaha Beach, which had a strong fighting force, many of the soldiers stationed on the Normandy coast were captured Russian and Polish soldiers and older Germans. Most of them did not want to fight. They were being forced to fight," said Christopher. "When the Allied Forces landed at Normandy, the German soldiers surrendered because they didn't really want to fight. In fact, if you look at the pictures of the captured soldiers, they were happy."

"Also, the Germans were unable to re-supply ammunition to many of the units on the front lines, forcing the Germans to either die or surrender," said Christopher.

"Are there any other missteps that you can think of?" questioned Sgt. Carney.

"One of the biggest problems the Allied soldiers faced was the landscape of the French countryside. They did not expect the hedgerows to be as high as they were. This was a failure in intelligence. The hedgerows provided excellent defensive positions for German soldiers and were almost impenetrable. Because there was only one opening to the field, the Germans would train guns on the entrance, wait until the Allied Forces got inside, and then gun them down. It took weeks before the Allies learned how to fight through the hedgerows. Also, these hedgerows caused massive casualties to the gliders when they landed and crashed into them," said Christopher.

"Go on," said Sgt. Carney.

"As the Allied Forces fought their way through France, it largely became a battle from field to field. Eventually, they figured out that if they attached steel teeth, like a garden rake, to the front of a tank, it made clearing the hedgerows easier and eliminated the Germans' strategic advantage. They also got through the hedgerows by blowing wide holes in them with TNT," stated Christopher.

"We should also remember that D-Day was just the beginning. Battles like the one fought at the Douve River footbridge took place all over the French countryside on D-Day as the Allied Forces attempted to accomplish their objectives. Small groups of soldiers fought battles originally designed for many more men—and they were fighting with men who, in many cases, they had never trained with. These battles raged throughout France for weeks as the Allied Forces strengthened their foothold, reconstituted their fighting units, and began to liberate France," declared Christopher.

"How would you evaluate the performance of the troops at D-Day?" asked Sgt. Carney.

"They're known as the 'Greatest Generation' for good reason," indicated Christopher. "Their generation came at a unique time in history. They were faced with fighting a war on two fronts: in the Pacific and in the Atlantic. Young men from across the country came together and fought in foreign lands for Freedom. They did so without reservation, and they believed in their cause. They trusted in God, and their faith sustained them through their darkest hours."

"The chaplains and medics were invaluable to the D-Day troops. In many ways, they sustained those who were injured or about to die. Captured medics helped not just

Allied troops but, also, injured Germans," said Christopher.

"Most important, the training, resilience, and resourcefulness of the young Allied soldiers were the defining factors in the outcome of the invasion. Despite a lack of leadership at the early stages of the invasion, due to the deaths of so many senior officers, enough men stepped up to lead. When they were lost, alone, or under enemy fire, they did not give up. When they were unable to accomplish their objective, they changed objectives and worked together. They wanted to survive, but, more than that, they also wanted to succeed because they believed in their mission," declared Christopher.

"Those who did survive are the old men you see marching down the street in Memorial Day parades. It is hard to picture them as vibrant young men fighting the Germans, however, they are the 'Greatest Generation' without a doubt. Everything we have is because of their sacrifices. Most of them don't talk about the war and never will. They carry battle scars that will never go away. They remember their friends who were killed in front of them, and they honor them by trying to live a good and decent life," stated Christopher.

"It is also important to remember that the 'Greatest Generation' applies to the entire generation—not just the men in battle. Their mothers, wives, and girlfriends went to work in factories, building the planes, ships, and guns used in the war effort to ensure they were successful. In many ways, they were the first generation of working women. The American people sacrificed at home to make sure 'their boys' had everything they needed to confront the enemy. Winning this war was a matter of necessity. Losing was not an option," declared Christopher.

"Americans bought war bonds to fund the effort despite not having much money. Hollywood made war movies that supported the troops and the war effort. Since there was no television, the public got their war news from newspapers and the newsreels at the beginning of movies. In fact, the media refused to publish photos of the D-Day aftermath for six months because they did not believe the American public could handle them," stated Christopher.

"Interesting," commented Sgt. Carney.

Private Frazier raised his hand. "Sergeant Carney, I still don't understand why we were involved in this war."

Shaking his head in disbelief, Sgt. Carney responded, "You will, son. Next week, we will cover the bombing of Pearl Harbor and the beginning of the war in the Pacific."

"Excellent job, Private Cosgrove," declared Sgt. Carney. "I didn't think you were paying attention. Class dismissed!"

As Christopher left the classroom, he was already looking forward to the following week: he and the Fighting Hawks would be together again at Pearl Harbor!

APPENDIX

Relevant Facts about D-Day

Although exact numbers are difficult to obtain because of the size of the invasion, as documented in *D-Day: 24 Hours That Saved the World* (TIME Magazine 2004) and *Overlord: D-Day and the Battle for Normandy* (Hastings 1984), the information below is roughly accurate.

Goal of Operation Overlord
First 24 hours, land:
      175,000 men
      1,500 tanks
      10,000 trucks

D-Day + 90 days, land:
      1.2 million men
      137,000 wheeled and semi-track vehicles
      4,217 full-track vehicles
      3,500 artillery pieces

Land Invasion
Total number of men landing on Normandy beaches: 156,000

By nationality:
>Americans: 58,000
>British, Canadian, Polish, and Dutch: 75,000

By beach assignment:
>Utah: 24,000 Americans
>Omaha: 25,000 Americans
>Gold: 25,000 Britons
>Juno: 24,000 Canadians and Britons
>Sword: 28,000 Britons

Number of ships in naval armada: >5,300
By type:
>Battleships: 9
>Cruisers: 23
>Destroyers: 104
>Corvettes: 71
>Minesweepers: >200
>Landing craft, various sizes: 2,700
>Submarines: 2

Air Invasion
Number of paratroopers/glider infantry landing in France: 24,000

Total number of paratroopers: 23,000
By nationality:
>American: 16,000
>British: 8,000

Total number of glider planes: 1,500
By nationality:

American: 1,200
British: 300

Number of planes in the air armada: >12,000
By type:
Heavy bombers: 3,467
Medium bombers: 1,645
Fighters: 5,409
C-47 transport planes: >900
Gliders with infantry and equipment: 1,500

By D-Day, 76,000 tons of bombs had been dropped on French railways.

Losses prior to D-Day:
Allied bombers: 3,000
Fighters: 1,500
Allied airmen killed or captured: 25,000

German Defenses on the Atlantic Wall

Concrete fortifications: >15,000
Harbor fortresses: several dozen large-caliber guns (155–240 mm)
Coastal batteries:
Medium-caliber guns (100–155 mm)
Resistance nests (*Widerstandnestern*): built into sea-wall, cliffs, and dunes; contained small-caliber guns (50–88 mm) positioned to ensure overlapping fields of fire on the beaches; nests included two pillbox fortifications with outside positions for machine guns, antiaircraft weapons, and mortars
Mines: >4 million, land and sea

Numerous sea and beach obstacles
"Asparagus": large wooden poles planted in fields to prevent glider landings
Flooding the low-lying areas in Normandy to drown paratroopers

Omaha Beach
Designated to land: 50,000 men

Landing troops: US 1st Division and 29th Division

Objective: Vierville, Colleville, and St. -Laurent

Of 32 amphibious tanks, 28 sank before reaching the shore

German defenses (all linked by trenches):
    Machine-gun nests: 85
    Rocket emplacements: 38
    Pillboxes: 35
    Antitank gun positions: 18
    Fortified gun batteries: 8
    Mortar pits: 6
    Field-artillery positions: 4

Beach defended by one division of young professional German soldiers

By 10:30 p.m., 30,000 men had landed at Omaha Beach

Total casualties: >2,000 soldiers

Utah Beach

Designated to land: 25,000 American troops

Landing troops: US 4th Division

Objective: Saint Martin, Saint-Germain, Pouppeville

Of 32 amphibious tanks, 28 reached the shore

German defenses: Russian POWs and older German soldiers

Total casualties: <200 missing, wounded, or killed

Gold Beach
Designated to land: 25,000 British troops

Landing troops: British 50th Division

Objective: Capture towns of Arromanches and Bayeux and link with US forces from Omaha Beach; hold critical crossroads in the town of Caen, eight miles inland

Total men landed by end of D-Day: 25,000

Total casualties approximately 400

Sword Beach
Landing troops: British 3rd Infantry Division; 178 free
French troops
Approximately 18,000 men

Objective: Link with British paratroopers (British 6th Airborne Division) farther inland and occupy critical cross-roads in the town of Caen, eight miles inland

Of 25 amphibious tanks, 21 reached shore (out of 40, 34 landed)

German defenses: One unit of German 21st Panzer Division

Total men landed by end of D-Day: 28,000

Total casualties: 214

Juno Beach
Designated to land: 9,000 British troops and 15,000 Canadian troops

Landing troops: British I Corp and 3rd Canadian Division

Objective: Saint-Aubin, Bernières, Courseulles-sur-Mer, and neighboring villages

Of 40 Centaur tanks, only 6 landed

Of 306 landing ships, 90 ships were destroyed by underwater mines

German defenses: machine-gun nests, snipers, fortified positions in town

Total men landed by end of D-Day: 21,400

Total vehicles landed: 3,200

Total casualties: 335 out of 1,000 soldiers

Estimated Total D-Day Casualties
        Americans: 3,000–5,000
        Britons: 2,500–3,000
        Canadians: <500

i.   *D-Day: 24 Hours That Saved The World* (New York: Time, Inc., Home Entertainment, 2004), p. 13.

ii. Ibid, p. 12.

iii. Quoted in Ian Gardner and Roger Day, *Tonight We Die as Men: The Untold Story of Third Battalion 506 Parachute Infantry Regiment from Toccoa to D-Day* (Oxford: Osprey Publishing, 2009), pp. 113–14. Prayer said by Lt. Col. Bob Wolverton to his men before embarking.

iv. As reported in Max Hastings, *Overlord: D-Day and the Battle For Normandy* (New York: Vintage Books, 1984), p. 80.

v. Gardner and Day, pp. 188–209.

REFERENCES AND
ACKNOWLEDGEMENTS

D-Day, June 6, 1944: The Climactic Battle of World War II
        By: Stephen E. Ambrose
        Published by: Simon & Schuster, 1994

Tonight We Die As Men: The Untold Story of Third Battalion 506
Parachute Infantry from Toccoa to D-Day
        By: Ian Gardner & Roger Day
        Published by: Osprey Publishing, 2009

Remember D-Day
        By: Ronald J. Drey
        Published by: National Geographic, 2004

D-Day: 24 Hours That Saved the World
        65th Anniversary Tribute
        Published by: Time Book Series, 2009

Overlord: D-Day and the Battle for Normandy
        By: Max Hastings
        Published by: Vintage Books, Random House, 1984

The Second World War: A Complete History
        By: Martin Gilbert
        Published by: Holt Paperbacks, 1989

All photos are reproduced courtesy of the National Archives.

http://www.army.mil/d-day/beaches.html

http://www.theholocaustexplained.org/ks3/the-final-solution/
german-expansionism/german-occupation-of-europe

http://www.ace-clipart.com/american-flag-photos-01.html

Made in the USA
Middletown, DE
29 January 2017